W9-BOL-514

For Nigel
and his
uncle David
—A.R.

For
Harriet Kasak
—P.M.

Grateful acknowledgement to Fumi Kosaka Davis
for providing the calligraphy.

Chip and the Karate Kick
Text copyright © 2004 by Anne Rockwell
Illustrations copyright © 2004 by Paul Meisel
Manufactured in China by South China Printing Company Ltd. All rights reserved.
www.harperchildrens.com

Library of Congress Cataloging-in-Publication Data
Rockwell, Anne F.
  Chip and the karate kick / by Anne Rockwell ; illustrated by Paul Meisel.
    p.   cm. — (Good sports)
  Summary: Chip starts taking karate lessons to be like the hero of his favorite television show, but his impatience
to earn a belt gets in the way of learning the true spirit of karate.
  ISBN 0-06-028442-0 —ISBN 0-06-028446-3 (lib. bdg.)
  [1. Karate—Fiction.   2. Patience—Fiction.   3. Rabbits—Fiction.   4. Animals—Fiction.]   I. Meisel, Paul, ill.   II. Title.
III. Good sports (HarperCollins)
PZ7.R5943 Ch 2004   [E]—dc21   CIP AC   2001024161
Typography by Matt Adamec
1 2 3 4 5 6 7 8 9 10
❖
First Edition

Chip and the
KARATE
KICK

by Anne Rockwell
illustrated by Paul Meisel

HARPERCOLLINS*PUBLISHERS*

Chip O'Hare wasn't very big, but he thought he was pretty tough. He wanted to be even tougher.

He wanted to be as tough as Striper Mee, whose TV show he never missed. He had a huge collection of Striper Mee action figures, Striper Mee trading cards, Striper Mee comics, and a big Striper Mee poster. Chip worked hard imitating things the world-famous martial-arts champion did—kicks, leaps, punches, karate chops, elbow strikes.

When a karate school opened in town, Chip was
the first to sign up. His parents bought him
a uniform called a *gi* with a long white belt to tie
around his waist.

On the first day of school Chip, Morgan, and Nina Jane arrived at the same time. Chip bounded into the classroom doing kicks, leaps, punches, and elbow strikes, making the sort of ferocious noises Striper Mee made.

Mr. Leo was the teacher. He wore a white *gi*, but his belt was black.

"Wow! Look at that! He's a black belt!" Chip said to Morgan and Nina Jane. "I can't wait to be one too! And you'll see—I will be soon."

"Good morning," Mr. Leo said to all the students. "I'm Mr. Leo—your *sensei* in the *dojo*."

"Huh? What's he talking about?" Chip asked Nina Jane.

"Be quiet and listen! Maybe you'll find out," she said.

sensei 先生

dojo 道場

"*Sensei* means 'teacher' in Japanese. *Dojo* means 'classroom,'" Mr. Leo said. "We use Japanese words for certain things here, because karate is an ancient martial art invented in Japan. I will tell you its story."

Chip groaned and sprawled across the carpet.
He never liked keeping still. He didn't want to listen
to a story. He was eager to start doing the things
Striper Mee did.

"Long ago," Mr. Leo said, "ordinary people on the island of Okinawa in Japan weren't allowed to have any weapons, although knights called *samurai* had sharp swords. Some *samurai* were bullies. People learned to defend themselves against them by inventing karate, which means 'empty fist.' Karate is a way of defending yourself without weapons, but it's <u>never</u> used to start a fight. Always remember that."

"First let's learn to sit with the eye of the tiger.
Sit still and quietly on the floor. Cross your legs.
Keep your back straight. Look me straight in the eye."

As they sat, Mr. Leo showed them how to take
slow, quiet, deep breaths. When Mr. Leo breathed in,
his stomach poked out. When he let out his breath,
his stomach poked in. He smiled as he breathed
slow and deep.

"Now let's learn to count to ten in Japanese," said Mr. Leo. "Repeat after me. *Ichi, ni, san, shi, go, roku, shichi, hachi, kyu, ju.*"

Then Mr. Leo showed the class how to do front kicks and back kicks. They counted as they kicked. "*Ichi, ni, san, shi, go, roku, shichi, hachi, kyu, ju.*"

"When are we going to break things with our bare hands like Striper Mee does?" Chip asked.

Mr. Leo smiled. "When you are ready."

1. Ichi 一   6. Roku 六

2. Ni 二   7. Shichi 七

3. San 三   8. Hachi 八

4. Shi 四   9. Kyu 九

5. Go 五   10. Ju 十

When class was over, Mr. Leo showed everyone how to bow. "From now on," he said, "each of you will work with a partner. You must bow to your partner when you begin practice and again when you finish. That is how you show respect for each other, even though you are opponents. Now please bow to your *sensei* to say good-bye."

As Chip walked home,
he wondered if Striper Mee
ever bowed to anyone.

At the start of each class Nina Jane
bowed to Chip. Sometimes Chip
remembered to bow back.
When he didn't, Nina Jane
wiggled her nose
to remind him.

In each class they learned something new. Mr. Leo taught them punching, kicking, side kicks and roundhouse kicks.

He taught them middle, high, and low blocks.
He taught them elbow strikes and *shuto*, the "knife
hand." Chip had seen Striper Mee break many things
with that, but he had always called it a karate chop.

Everyone in class shouted *"Hite!"* as they kicked
and punched. They counted, *"Ichi, ni, san, shi, go,
roku, shichi, hachi, kyu, ju,"* during their drills.

On the day of the tournament, everyone's parents came to watch.

Chip went first. He shouted *"Hite!"* and broke a wooden board using *shuto*.

"Now do I get a yellow belt?" he asked Mr. Leo.

Mr. Leo smiled. "When you are ready."

Chip didn't understand. Nina Jane already had a yellow belt. Brendan did too. Chip <u>knew</u> he was better at karate than they were.

When it was time for his next karate class,
Chip didn't want to go. He was mad because Mr. Leo
hadn't given him a yellow belt. How was he going to
get a black belt if he didn't even have a yellow one?
He knew he had to get a yellow one, then orange, blue,
green, and brown, before he could get a black one.

It was taking too long!

Chip went to the park at the end of his block.
His neighbor, Melissa Bunny, was there, trying to fly
her kite. Chip never played with Melissa. She was
too little to do the things he liked to do.

Soon Bernie Bullie came to the park. Chip never
played with him, either. He was too big and mean.

Bernie grabbed the kite from Melissa. He laughed
when she started crying.

Chip tried to grab the kite from Bernie, but big, tough Bernie Bullie wouldn't let go. "Nyah, nyah! Just try and take it, pip-squeak!" said Bernie.

He held on to the kite and kicked Chip. Chip was about to kick Bernie back when he had an idea.

"Have it your way," Chip said to Bernie. "But first
I have to warm up." He breathed deeply as Mr. Leo
had taught him. He looked straight at Bernie with
the eye of the tiger.

Bernie's mouth fell open as Chip shouted, *"Hite!"* and gave a great roundhouse kick through the air. *"Hite!"* Chip made *shuto* as he aimed a front kick toward Bernie. Bernie was so scared, he dropped the kite and ran away.

Chip grabbed the kite and gave it to Melissa. They took turns flying it. Then they walked home together.

"You sure are good at karate," Melissa said.

"Thanks," said Chip. "I've been taking lessons. My *sensei*—that means 'teacher'—has a black belt. You should see <u>him</u> do *shuto*!"

That night at the Bunny family cookout, Chip saw Mr. Leo talking with Melissa.

They talked for a long time.

Chip decided to go back to his *dojo* the next day.

This time Nina Jane didn't have to remind him to bow. At the end of the class Mr. Leo bowed to Chip. He handed him a brand-new yellow belt to wear with his *gi.*

"Well done, Chip," said Mr. Leo. "By helping Melissa, you showed that you are learning the spirit of karate. Your way to the black belt has truly begun."

"Wow!" Chip said as he proudly tied it around his waist. "Thanks, *sensei*-o!"